BY

The ABC's of Making Good Choices

MRS. GOOD CHOICE SERIES

Amelia's Agreeable Attitude

Benjamin's Belligerent Bandit

Christian's Complimentary Contribution

Diego's Damaged Dinosaur

Emily and Elijah's Extraordinary Experience

Faith and Frisky's Fascinating Friendship

♥

II

"Teach Children to be HONEST with the Help of Mrs. Good Choice!"

"How many of us have heard the old saying: *Honesty is always the best policy?* My wish for our younger generation is that they always tell the truth. In handing this value down, our world becomes a better place. The key question is: *How can we teach such a valuable character trait?* Research shows that children ages 3-5 years often tell untruths. It takes time for them to distinguish between real world and fantasy …"

THE PROVIDER – In The Classroom (September 2014) **www.pgcfcaa.com** (Prince George's County Family Child Care Association, Inc.)

♥

IV

"Upon meeting Dawn Young she advised me that there are two things that she could not do: drive and play tennis. After working with her, I think she may be wrong, and with the advances in technology, she will virtually do both. I found no evidence of her limitation when it came to leading, motivating, inspiring, and achieving. As an elementary school principal, Mrs. Young passionately advocated for every child."

Roger Bynum, Retired
Exemplary Educator Program
Appalachia Educational Laboratory
Corporate Vice-President
Tennessee Department of
Education

♥

"There are only a few people in this world who have the ability to lift your spirits and encourage you to be more thankful with only a few words such as, "Hello, I'm Mrs. Good Choice!" Dawn Young is that kind of person. From the first moment I met her at a homeschool convention, I knew we would be best friends forever. She is energetic, highly motivated, and a genuine educator. If she writes a book, read it. If she starts a Facebook group, join it. If she speaks at a live event, attend it. Stay as close to her as you can and you will be blessed. She is one of a kind."

Rhea Perry
Educating For Success, Inc. - CEO
♥

"On behalf of the third and fourth grade-tutoring group at East Cheatham Elementary School, we would like to thank Mrs. Dawn Young for sharing her character program with us. Through Mrs. Young's program, she provides a foundation of needed growth for students to become productive citizens. Not only are Mrs. Young's character books filled with relevant information, they also provide real-life experiences. The relationships built within the classroom result in more connection to others in the learning environment."

East Cheatham Elementary School Third and Fourth Grade Tutoring Group.

♥

x

"Writing an ABC book about good choices makes it easy for kids to learn!"
… Dailynn, third grade

"I am glad she wrote the book. It will help kids learn to make good choices."
… Kate, third grade

"I like the fact that children can learn about good choices while they are young."
… Madelyn, third grade

"All big kids need to share this book with little kids. Even a 20-year-old can learn something from it!"
… McKinleigh, third grade

♥

♥

My World of Light and Love ... ... by Dawn

By Dawn Cowley Young, Ed.S

♥

My World of Light and Love by Dawn

Jay M. Horne, Digital Art Production

Cindy L. Martin, Editor

Cataloguing Publication Data

Young, Dawn.

My World of Light and Love by Dawn / Dawn C. Young

ISBN: 978-0-9912326-7-3

Library of Congress Control Number: 2015905008

Bookflurry.com

New Port Richey, FL

XVI

To my wonderful parents, Don &
Mary Cowley, who raised me, a legally
blind daughter, with love, care, and
high expectations. I thank them for
teaching me the meaning of hard work,
good character, and giving me the
determination to accomplish anything I
set my heart out to do.

To my phenomenal husband, Steve,
who loves and completes me. I love you.

D.Y.

♥

XVIII

ACKNOWLEDGMENTS

I first would like to thank all my readers!

Thank you also to Jay Horne, who made this project come to life.

I would like to give a special thank you to my very own Line Tamer—Cindy Martin—my wonderful editor.

♥

Table of Contents

XXII

Chapter 1
The Beginning
♥

'You don't miss what you never had!' is one of my favorite sayings. My name is Dawn Renee Cowley Young. I was raised in a small rural town in Magnolia, Ohio and I am the oldest child of Donald and Mary Cowley. I was taught at a very young age to have perseverance. Giving up was not an option.

♥

I was born legally blind with vision that could not be corrected with glasses. My parents took me to an optometrist at the age of three and the only letter I could read on the eye chart was the giant 'E'. It was strongly suggested that I would need to go to the Sight

Saving School for Blind Children. Fate stepped in and made sure I was not enrolled there, and I am so thankful for that! My life was, and is, as rich and full as I could ever imagine. As you read on, you will see that I have wanted for nothing; indeed, I am blessed to have skills some fully sighted individuals don't have.

When I was four-and-a-half-years-old, I received my very own baby doll … my brother—David Scott Cowley. Mom said I was a good big sister. I adored Dave then and still do, today.

Dave and I were blessed with hard-working, honest, loving parents. My mom and dad encouraged us to work hard, always do our best, and never give up. My parents weren't rich in money, but very wealthy in sharing their love and good advice.

Growing up in a small place had its advantages. Our town of Magnolia had a population of less than a thousand people. The town had one gas station, one red light, a pharmacy (my mom and five of my uncles were born in this building), and nice sidewalks.

My mom was a bit over-protective. I think she would have been this way even if I had been born with 20/20 vision. The example that comes to my mind regarding over-protection is when I look at home movies of myself roller-skating on a nice sidewalk outside our house.

They show me skating with only one skate. My other leg is covered with bruises and scabs. When I questioned my mom about the movies, she told me she only allowed me to wear one skate at a time. She said she didn't want me to hurt myself.

Now, it all makes sense to me. Who wouldn't look like a battered child if they were only given one skate? *Off balance!* 'Mom, what were you thinking?' I chuckle every time I see this. Vision had nothing to do with my skating or injuries. Someone should have taught me how to balance on one foot.

While I am talking about sidewalks, I remember being thrilled when I was probably in the second grade and given permission to walk around *two* town blocks and not just *one*. Many of my childhood friends were granted permission way before me, but that permission was withheld out of love.

Luckily (for me), one set of my grandparents lived three doors down from us. I was allowed to walk there on my own, which included crossing a small alley.

♥

Magnolia Elementary School is where I attended first through fourth grades. When I was five-years-old, I attended kindergarten at the Magnolia United Methodist Church. I remember many of my classmates and fun activities that we completed. However, one activity got me into trouble. I refused to finger paint! My teacher called my parents and reported my behavior. Refusing to finger paint had nothing to do with my vision ... I just didn't want to get my hands dirty.

While this made perfect sense to me, I learned at an early age that I was to do whatever my teacher told me. My parents taught me to show respect, always, and to be honest. Life was not always fair and things were not always going to go my way!

Learning for me was auditory rather than visual, for the most part. When we find ourselves in the circumstance of having to live without one or more of our physical senses, the capabilities of our remaining senses can develop at an alarming rate. My hearing is phenomenal. Most people can hear as low as twenty decibels. I can hear as low as five decibels. When the school nurses checked my hearing along with my other classmates, they were always amazed.

My elementary school teachers were very accommodating to my needs. I could never read the writing on the chalkboard, even if I was seated in the front row. Teachers allowed me to push my desk up against the board or walk up to it when I needed to see something. I guess I could *try* to blame my poor spelling on this ... but I am not making excuses for myself. All I can say is—thank goodness for technology and spell check!

♥

One incident comes to mind in second grade involving the chalkboard. My mom had sewn me a new wrap around skirt for school. Mrs. Brinkman, my second grade teacher, was teaching a lesson and had asked some boys to push my desk up to the chalkboard.

When the lesson was over, I got up to push my desk back into place. My new skirt got hooked on the side of my desk … off it came! Mrs. Brinkman handled the situation so nicely.

In a calm voice, she said, "Gather around girls, gather around."

It could only happen to me!

♥

As a child, I loved performing. Not that I was graceful or talented, but in my mind there was no question ... I *was*. In the second grade, I played one of a group of Dutch Girls Dancers. We had real costumes and everything. My feet were too big to fit into the real wooden shoes—disappointing, but not the end of the world.

In the third grade, my friends were chosen to be snowflakes in a play. The teacher told me I was much too clumsy. It hurt my feelings, but life went on! I ended up singing in the chorus.

♥

My fond memories of elementary school and the wonderful teachers who *did* treat me in a kind way (which were the majority), are the reasons I have spent the last 28 years of my life in education. I am so thankful for the choices made and the path that my parents chose for me. Thank you, Mom and Dad!

♥

Daddy's Girl

Dawn at Three Months
Cutie Pie

Girly Girl

an mills

My First Birthday
1959

Here Kitty Kitty

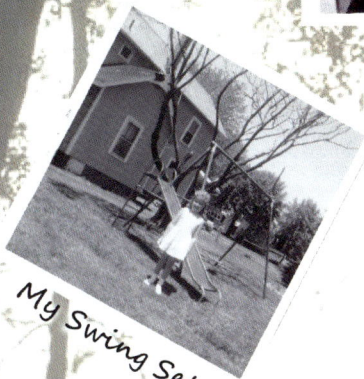

Good
Big
Sister

My Swing Set

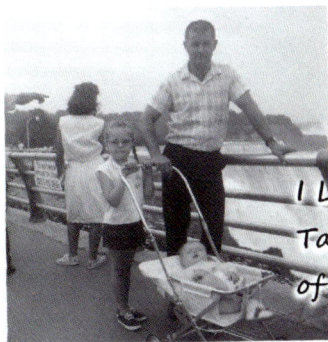

I Liked to Help
Take Care
of Dave

First Grade

Third Grade

Sixth Grade

Tenth Grade

Senior Picture
1976

School
Days

High School
Graduation

Chapter 2
Lasting Friendships
♥

I learned at a very early age of the things I treasure most—people and friendships. Making friends and meeting people have always come easily to me. It is another great gift that God blessed me with instead of 20/20 vision. When I think back to my early childhood, I was blessed with great friends. Gina and Jimmy were two of my early childhood friends and neighbors.

Jimmy (last name James) lived across the street from us. He had three siblings and his parents owned our local grocery store. His mom was one of my high school English teachers. According to my mom, I always insisted that I was going to marry Jimmy when we grew up, but he told me he couldn't marry me because he was planning on marrying another friend of ours, Mary Kay. Life happened and that marriage did not. Neither did mine and Jimmy's marriage, but we did go through elementary, middle and high school with each other and attended my junior prom together. Judge James David James of the Family Court still lives in Magnolia with his own family.

Gina Barheimer was one of my best friends in early elementary school. She, her parents, and three older sisters lived next door to my Grandma and Grandpa Marlor. We spent much time playing outside and at each other's houses.

I had many, many other friends while I was growing up … they all hold a special place in my heart and in my memories.

My cousin Cindi and I were very close as we were growing up. Her dad and mine were brothers. I was a year older, but we always got along great. She was like the sister to me that I never had. I think I was like her sister too, as she had two brothers of her own. What is interesting to me is that we grew up and both went into education, became teachers, and elementary school principals. All those years of playing school paid off!

♥

I am very blessed to have so many great friends. I always say I have two BFFs—one from Ohio and one from Tennessee. My Ohio best friend is Terri Sue Mitzel Surbey. Our relationship goes back before kindergarten. Our parents became friends first. We have always had a natural, honest, heartwarming friendship. Terri is smart, beautiful, caring and, most of all, the person that probably knows more about me than any other person in this world. Although we live in two different states … Ohio and Tennessee … our friendship has existed over fifty years.

My Tennessee BFF is Sherry Elaine Whited Thomas. I met Sherry in 1992 at East Cheatham Elementary School. It was my first day to teach the fifth grade there and Sherry's daughter was in that same grade level. Sherry came up to me and introduced herself. We formed an instant friendship. Sherry is kind, hardworking, pretty, and one of the most honest and loyal people I know.

Sherry and her wonderful husband, Nicky, along with their two children became part of my family away from home. Sherry's three grandsons call me *Granny Dawn*. 22 years later, we are still very close.

One of the most amazing things is now Terri and Sherry have become friends! I introduced them several years ago on one of Terri's Tennessee visits. The three of us have shared some great times and made lasting memories. Friends are the things in my life I treasure the most.

Over the years, I have realized that I can get along with anyone. I respect people! It doesn't matter to me what country they were born in, what their economic situation is, or what type of personality they exhibit. I value every person I meet and respect them for who they are on the inside. God created each of us in a unique and different way.

Facebook has been a wonderful tool to use for keeping up with old friends and classmates. I've met hundreds of people.

A friend on Facebook asked me recently, 'If you came with a label, what would your label read?'

I responded, 'I love to talk to strangers!'

♥

Prom King & Queen
May 1976

Loving
Parents

Dad's Surprise 80th
Birthday Party

Nice Looking Couple

Merry Christmas

Then & Now

Cousins, Denny and Cindi Cowley. I am in the middle!

Two Principals
October 2014

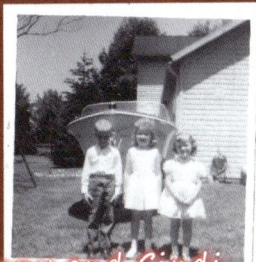

My BFF Terri and I
with our siblings

Forever Friends

1999

CHEERS

October 2014

Best Friends

My BFF Sherry
always ready to HELP

My two BFFs
SHOPPING FUN

Surprise Party for
BFF Sherry

Chapter 3
When life hands you lemons … make lemonade … Cowley's Lemonade!
♥

My dad learned the meaning of hard work as a boy living on a farm. He was the third from the oldest in a family with twelve siblings. My mom had five brothers and one sister. She was used to working hard, too. I talked earlier about my parents teaching my brother and myself the meaning of hard work. Here is the story:

In 1967, Dad was an industrial engineer. One of his co-workers offered him a chance to make some extra money selling lemonade at the Magnolia Homecoming. My mom was very skeptical and even laughed at the idea. However, when she saw the golden opportunity of people loving the fresh lemonade and their willingness to buy it, she was in.

That was the beginning of *Cowley's Lemonade* business. Each cup came with a hand-squeezed half of a lemon, sugar, ice, and water and had to be shaken by hand. Each cup was only 25 cents back then. After much trial and error with Dad trying to work a full-time job, Mom running the household, taking care of my brother and me, attending local carnivals and homecomings selling lemonade—it was obvious that something needed to change.

♥

We all decided it was time for Dad to quit his job and sell lemonade full time with the help of his family. Obviously, God's hand was in it all. My family continued with lemonade concession stands that we took to carnivals and county fairs. I was only eight-years-old when this family business began.

Each summer we traveled from place-to-place, setting up our stands for a week at a time. We traveled to fairs in Ohio and Pennsylvania, living in our motor home. We attended the same events each year. Even though it was a hardship giving up our summer breaks to work in the business, I can also say it was a blessing.

My family has met some incredible people over the years. Many have turned into lifetime friends. My brother and I worked very hard each summer but the benefits were worth it. We both were able to attend college without student loans to pay back. I continued working and helping my family each summer until I turned 29 and moved to Tennessee.

My family's lemonade business enabled me to become more outgoing and allowed me to develop great people skills along with a solid work ethic … all wonderful personality builders! When you work in a job dealing with all types of people, day in and day out, something good *can* come out of it.

Cowley's Lemonade is still in existence. My brother, Dave, became a middle school teacher and purchased the business from my parents. He still goes to five fairs every summer. My family proved that the saying: *When life hands you lemons, make LEMONADE*—really can become a reality.

♥

Our First Lemonade Stand
I am Squeezing Lemons

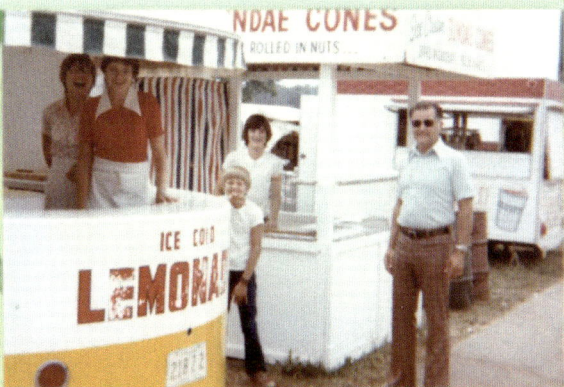

Terri, Dave, Dad and I

Chapter 4
Where there was a will … I found a way
♥

When I say that I am legally blind, most people are amazed that I *can* do all that I do. There are only two things I always say that I *can't* do … drive a car and play tennis.

Allow me to clarify; I know how to operate a car. As a teenager, my dad took me out on back dirt roads and allowed me to prove this point more than once. I also drove a friend's car in my driveway. Sometimes, when high school got out, my friend, Carol, would let me drive her VW bug (one of the old ones, those of us of a certain age … cough, cough … will remember) down the long, blacktop driveway to our house. It was about a hundred yards long and I would honk the horn to let everyone know I was driving and on my way! Also, I wanted to let all who heard know just how cool I was.

As far as tennis is concerned, who wants to be hit with a ball? Not this girl! Well, I *did* make an exception once. I have a cute story you will read about in another chapter about my 'no tennis playing' and my soul mate, Steve.

♥

I have always had a wonderful attitude and willingness to try new things. I am not afraid of much. As a child in PE class, I was not athletic. But, boy, would I give it my all! If the class was playing softball, the teacher picked another student to bat for me and I would run to the bases. I was very fast.

At family picnics, my family modified softball for my benefit. We called the game Elephant Ball. We used a regular bat and one of the big plastic balls about twenty inches in diameter. My dad and I were always the opposing pitchers. I could hit the fire out of an Elephant Ball.

♥

In middle school, I decided I wanted to join the gymnastics team. My middle name is Renee—*not* Grace. My first try on the balance beam … I fell on the teacher. The parallel bars and vault were not my strong points. My coach decided that floor exercise was my best fit. I practiced and practiced a routine developed just for me.

The day of the first meet found me excited and nervous. I

performed and even received a ribbon for my efforts. However, my overall score was 3.25 out of a 10 and I received a yellow ribbon … pink was the worst. I would love to have a home movie of my routine. I am sure it would consist of a long-legged blonde flopping all over the floor. I laugh just thinking about it!

♥

My parents always supported and encouraged me to try to do all of the things that interested me. I only remember one time when my dad said he didn't think I should go for something that I was eager to try. A group of my friends were going to go snow-skiing and I wanted to go along and try it out.

My family was planning a trip to Florida the following week. My dad asked me how I would feel about sitting on the beach with a cast on my leg. Of course, the choice was mine to make—no pressure there! I chose to follow my dad's advice. Unbelievably, Mom—over-protective as she was—had decided to let me go on the trip.

In high school, I decided to join the track team. When I tried the hurdles (not very successfully), I always knocked them over. My first attempt at the long jump, I landed in the sandpit—face first. Then, I thought that the mile relay just might be an event I could handle.

While practicing the relay with three other teammates, the coach asked, "Who was the third person in that relay?"

I replied, "It was me, Coach!" He proceeded to tell me that my arms were flopping around like a chicken.

♥

My vision has never held me back because I live by faith, not by sight. I know how to swim, dive off a diving board, roller-skate (with *two* skates), bowl (can't see the pins, don't need to!), love to dance, and even ride a bike. I have white water rafted the Ocoee River and been tubing. As a child, we always went sled riding on a huge dike by our house. I was fearless!

One time, as an adult, I did bite off a little more than I could chew. I was out in Colorado for an educational conference. A friend and I decided that we would try riding a bike down the Rocky Mountains. I was willing to try it. I *knew* I could handle a bike.

Well, let me specify a few things. First, we had to ride a ski lift to the top of the mountain. Next issue; I only knew how to ride a bike with brakes controlled by the pedals, not hand brakes on the handlebars. Oh boy, *then* I forgot I had to wear the crazy helmet … which did a nice job of smashing my hair.

Biggest mistake, somehow we ended up on the advanced trail and not the beginner's trail. The entire four-hour ride my friend was in front of me yelling, "Rock on the left—rock on the right!" I made it safe and sound, and am here telling you the story. Thank you, God!

♥

I am here to tell you if you *think* you can, *YOU CAN*! If I had allowed my vision to stand in the way, I would not be the person I am today!

♥

Never Hold Back

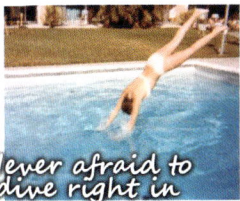

Never afraid to
dive right in

Me Driving
January 1981

Catch of the Day

Dancing Queen
1990

Young Bathing
Beauty

Chapter 5
Dave's Sister VS Dawn's Brother
♥

I graduated from Sandy Valley High School in 1976. My high school days were filled with fun, friendships, and lasting memories. I loved to get involved in extra-curricular activities and have tons of friends.

Remember my level of 'grace' from floor exercise? Although I was never a cheerleader, it did not keep me from trying out each year. During my freshman year I was our school mascot, the Cardinal Bird.

I loved making the crowds at football and basketball games laugh with my crazy antics. I may not have been a cheerleader, but I found a way to hang out with my cheerleader friends. I had a lot of fun in the process.

During my high school years, I served on the Yearbook Staff, Pep Club, Student Council, Future Homemakers Club, and many other clubs. I was very involved in the high school choir, and even sang in a couple of select groups from within the choir. My classmates voted for Senior Prom Queen; one of my fondest highlights was winning. It was a wonderful way to end my senior year.

My grades in high school were average and above. I am sure if I had socialized *less* and applied myself *more* I could have received straight A's.

Once again, my life was not about being legally blind; it was about socializing with people and finding a way to contribute to society while achieving personal fulfillment.

♥

After graduating from high school, I wasn't quite ready to attend college. I always say I was a 'late bloomer'. I decided to attend college in 1982. My brother, Dave, graduated from high school in 1981. He signed up to attend Kent State Stark Campus and commute from home. He attended the first semester by himself.

Then Dave became a lucky guy—his big sister decided to sign up and attend Kent State by his side. I began my first semester at Kent State Stark Campus in January of 1982. I had my own chauffeur—

my little brother. All of Dave's friends knew me as 'Dave's sister'.

My decision to major in elementary education was one of the best ones I have ever made. With hard work, perseverance, and determination I became a nontraditional student at the age of 24. Most of my friends were graduating from college and here I was just beginning my journey. Better late than never!

♥

Inner Faith Campus Ministry was the first job that I had with no connection to family. I worked on campus about twenty hours a week as a secretary for a wonderful Methodist minister and Catholic sister.

Essentially, I was more of a PR person than a secretary. This was a great place where students could come for counseling, to drink coffee, and study.

In addition, this is where I met my first husband, Jeff Vincent. After dating for three-and-a-half-years, we married and moved to Tennessee. Fifteen years later, we parted as friends and went in two different directions. Jeff has remarried and I wish him much happiness. He was a part of my life for almost 19 years and, of course, that cannot change. I would not want it to, as 'Mrs. Dawn Vincent' played a part in shaping me into the person I am today; just as the rest of my experiences have.

I soon changed the perception of just being 'Dave's sister'. Being the take-charge person I am, I decided to get involved in Student Government. Serving as Student Body President for two years connected me with hundreds of students and faculty. My little brother, Dave, became known as 'Dawn's brother' … in a very short time.

In 1986, my brother married an amazing girl … Mary Ann. She is the best sister-in-law a gal could ask for. I actually met her *before* Dave did, when they met at college. I am godmother to their daughter, my beautiful, talented, sweet 22-year-old niece. Although we live a long way from each other, I have managed to be at many of her dance recitals, birthdays, and graduations over the years. My brother says she acts just like me. *Go figure!*

♥

1976

My Little Brother

Say Cheese

Dave's Sister
vs.
Dawn's Brother

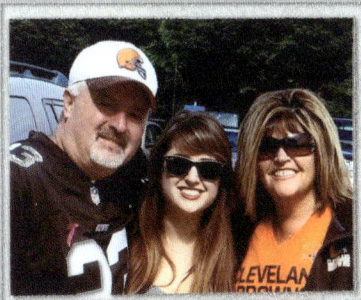

My Brother Dave, Niece Rachel,
and Sister-in-Law Mary Ann.

Kent Stark
Associate Graduation
1984

SANDY VALLEY
HIGH SCHOOL

Chapter 6
Teacher Talk
♥

I graduated from Kent State University in 1986, ten years after graduating from high school. My first teaching job was teaching the fifth and sixth grade language arts at St. James Elementary School in Waynesburg, Ohio. My second year of teaching found me teaching the fourth grade.

After moving to the south in 1988, I was hired to teach sixth, seventh, and eighth grade math at St. Pius X in Nashville, Tennessee. I made wonderful friends and built positive relationships in the four years that I taught there.

My next six years of teaching the fourth and fifth grades were at East Cheatham Elementary School in Ashland City, Tennessee. I can honestly say that in my twelve years of teaching, I never had a parent question me about my vision.

♥

Children are very resilient. I always explained to my classes at the beginning of each year, 'You will notice something about me. You will notice that when I read, I hold the books very close in order to see the print.' I would explain that this is just the way God made me.

Once again, when we must live without a physical sense most other people take for granted, I believe God helps us compensate for this. My classroom management skills were tremendous. This was not because I *saw* everything going on in the classroom, but because I could *hear* every word spoken.

In 1992, I decided to attend Trevecca Nazarene College. I graduated in 1994 with a Masters in Administration and Supervision. I applied for several administrative jobs once I finished my degree. I believe our destinies are already planned for us, and I believe that this was part of the destiny God had in mind for me.

My principal at East Cheatham Elementary was chosen to open a new high school in our district. This left a principal vacancy at my school. Three people applied for the job. I was the lucky candidate. In 1998, I became an elementary school principal of a K-4 school with about 500 students.

Being a principal is a very hard job, but it is probably my favorite position in which I served. Remember, I value people, and I was a hands-on principal. Every decision I made was based on what was best for the students. This is where I began gaining the largest part of my love of teaching children *to make good choices*.

♥

I have taken a few sign language classes over the years. I had three very sweet deaf children at my school when I was principal. I wanted to be able to communicate with them. It was difficult for me to learn because I have a hard time seeing the signs if I am not close enough to the person signing. I know a few basic signs, though.

I have also been able to witness the use of a Braillewriter. A vision-impaired teacher who served students in my school while I was principal introduced me to one. Although it seems very difficult to learn, I would like to do so, someday.

In a school of 70 employees, 500 children and hundreds of moms, dads, grandparents, and other guardians, I have met so many wonderful people. I served as principal for 13 years. When I thought about my journey as a principal, I realized that my first kindergarten class (that began school when I began teaching) graduated the same year that I finished my job as principal.

I always encouraged my teachers, assistants, and students to be lifelong learners. It is important to lead by example. I attended Austin Peay State University and graduated with an Educational Specialist Degree in 2004. My area of study was Character Education.

Throughout my years as a principal, I had two school mottos: *'Character Counts'* and *'No Matter Where You Go or What You Do, Make Good Choices!'*

I believe that early intervention is the key to teaching our children the importance of what they can do to live a happy and successful life. My passion for teaching children to make wise choices still guides my work today.

During my last three years in education, I served as a Teacher Improvement Coordinator for 12 schools in our county. Within that time, I was fortunate to work and evaluate hundreds of K-12 teachers. My job was to coach and help improve instruction for students. It was a rewarding job because I was still doing what was best for students.

After all of this teacher talk, just think how different my life would have been if my parents had sent me to the Sight Saving School for Blind Children. This school was and is a wonderful place for those who need it, but I just didn't. God had a plan for me that did not include that school.

♥

Principal Dawn Vincent
2000 - 2001

Teacher Mode
East Cheatham Elementary

Teacher

1994

Principal

2004

SEPTEMBER 1, 2000

Best Ways to Prevent Cancer Page 38

Woman's Day

Free Poster
Foods That Keep You Healthy
Plus a Week of Menus

Lose Weight for Good
With These Simple Tricks

580
best-ever
tips, solutions, recipe

it's time to go back to school

kids'day

Teachers' Best
Back-to-School
Advice

Pasta Primavera
Page 123

"Establish a regular bedtime before school starts, then stick to it.

Dawn R. Vincent Many children come to school sleepy, and are unable to follow directions or absorb the day's lessons."

Dawn R. Vincent, principal, East Cheatham Elementary School, Ashland City, TN

xpert's **rites**

School's O
How to Make It
The Best Year Eve
See Page 125

TMAS FAIR BESTSELLERS

ND LESS, SAVE MORE: 27 TIPS

16 WAYS TO GET THE MOST OUT OF LIFE

www.womansday.com

$1.49

Our Principal

Mrs. Dawn Young

Another Day At Work

Walking Track
Ceremony

Fall Festival
Fun

2008 - 2009

Chapter Seven
Touched by an Angel
♥

After living on my own for three years, in 2005 I met my soul mate, Steven Lyle Young. Our story is fun, unbelievable, and touching. Do you believe that God works miracles? Do you think God can unite two people from two different states … with the help of an angel … in a casino? We do! Here is the story:

My parents came down from Ohio for a weeklong visit in 2005. It was Valentine's Day weekend. We decided to make a visit to Metropolis, IL—home of Superman. We went not to celebrate Superman, but to stay at a casino for the weekend. Dad likes to shoot Craps. My mom and I like to play Black Jack. Yes, I *am* legally blind, but I can still see the cards.

My idea of playing Black Jack is socializing with the other people at the table. Of course, being the outgoing person I am, I am usually the person to start conversations. It is just who I am and what I do. My opening line for most people is "Where are you from?"

On Friday night, Steve was playing at our table, but I didn't even notice him. He was talking with an elderly gentleman who was sitting on the end beside him most of the night.

On Saturday, I returned to the same table to play. This time, Steve was sitting on my right. I asked him where he was from. He told me he was from Birmingham, AL. He asked me where I was from and what I did for a living. I told him Nashville along with the other details. He asked me if I was married. I told him I had been divorced for three years. I asked him the same question. He told me he had been alone for a long time.

♥

Now the fun question; do you remember what the two things I always tell people I don't do? He asked me if I played tennis. I told him the same thing I tell others, that I am legally blind, and there are two things I don't do—drive or play tennis. We spent the afternoon chit- chatting and flirting with each other. Good thing I *wasn't* driving because I just *know* something akin to an angelic tennis ball smacked both of us upside the head. It was **magic**.

♥

He was staying with friends in Paducah, KY for the weekend. When he was ready to leave, he asked me for my number. He asked if he could stop by my school to take me for lunch the following week.

On Sunday, Mom, Dad, and I returned to the casino for one more day. We had just arrived when Mom asked me, "Do you think your friend will be here today?" Before I could answer, she said. "Here he comes."

Steve had come back to spend time with me. We decided not to gamble at all on Sunday. We spent time just talking and getting acquainted. I learned that Steve had become a widower at an early age. He raised his son, Fred, on his own for eighteen years. This confirmed my feelings that this was a good man. In our conversation, Steve asked me if I had noticed the man he was talking to on Friday night. He said that they had talked and he thought they had bonded. Interestingly, the same man was sitting in the same seat on Saturday watching the interaction between the two of us. Steve said he tried several times to make eye contact with the older gentleman, but the man totally ignored him.

Here is the best part of the story. When the gentleman stood up to leave, he looked Steve right in the eye … and winked. Steve said he had goose bumps. It was almost as if the man was saying, 'My work here is finished.' We both feel as though our meeting was caused by divine intervention.

♥

Although Steve said the weekend was his worst loss, money wise, he says it is also his best win, because he met me. It is not often that a guy meets his future in-laws on the same day he meets his future wife.

He did come by my school the following Tuesday and took me to lunch. We began dating and entered into a long distance relationship. By July … we were engaged. On February 11, 2006 … we were married. Our marriage was exactly one year from the date that we met.

We are now living our 'happily ever after', and we both feel as though our lives were *touched by an angel* and I knew I had found my very own *Superman.*

♥

My
Sweet
Family

Feb. 11, 2006
My soulmate
"Steve"

Fred and Shu's Wedding
Oct. 20, 2014

Fred's College
Graduation

My Sweet
Son

Chapter 8
Fun Junkies
♥

The last nine years of my life have been wonderful. A big thank you goes to my awesome husband, Steve. We are so compatible in our values, the things we like to do, and making each other laugh. I think if you can laugh together, it can make any relationship fun and lasting.

Steve is such a thoughtful, caring, over-protective husband. My vision problem never made him hesitate to get involved in our relationship. He is constantly trying to be my eyes. I am very thankful and feel blessed for his care and concern, but I am very independent. Many times, I try to lovingly ignore his help.

When I married Steve, I also became the stepmom to an amazing son, Fred. Fred is smart, creative, and so much like his dad, it is almost scary. I remember meeting Fred for the first time. He was a junior in college.

We had met for a fun Saturday of Putt Putt Golf and lunch. When Fred found out that I was an elementary school principal he said, "I think you and my dad will get along great because he is very elementary." He also replied, "I need you, too!" I knew then that I was in love with two guys—instead of one.

♥

Last October, we also gained a wonderful daughter-in-law, Shu. Shu is intelligent, pretty, and great at giving Fred a run for his money.

We love our son and daughter-in-law, but dislike that they live so far away. They live in Los Angeles, CA. We try to visit as often as possible.

Steve and I both love to travel. I have traveled more in the last nine years then I did my first 45 years of life. My husband is the best trip planner. He researches and finds the most amazing things for us to do at each destination.

For my 50th birthday, Steve planned a trip to Venice, Italy. It was so much fun. The bread and wine were enough for me to want to move there. We took a train to visit Austria for a couple of days.

My favorite movie in the whole world is *Sound of Music.* I wanted to grow up and be just like

Maria. I have probably watched the movie more than thirty times in my life. I also know all of the words of each song.

As a wonderful surprise, Steve planned a *Sound of Music Tour* in Austria. It was so amazing to be in the place and see the beautiful scenery of the filming locations of the movie. The two of us have made so many beautiful memories and there are many more to come!

♥

I have always been a fan of Donny and Marie Osmond. One year, Steve purchased a front row ticket in Las Vegas for me to attend the Donny and Marie Show. It came with a chance to meet and greet them both after the show. It was so much fun getting to meet my first love, *Donny Osmond*. Donny and

Marie both signed their books for me and we had a photo taken together.

Most of our vacations include the ocean and a beach. Over the years, we have been on numerous cruises, visited many islands, and made some wonderful friends in the process.

We both enjoy going to movies, theater, and concerts. However, we do not have to go anywhere to have fun together. We enjoy staying home and watching TV. Just spending quality time with one another is what makes me the happiest.

♥

Steve's sister, Marsha, named us 'Fun Junkies'. I love the name. I am blessed beyond what I deserve—to have met my soul mate

at the age of 47. I never dreamed
that I could be so happy this late in
life.

♥

Flamingo

Donny & Marie

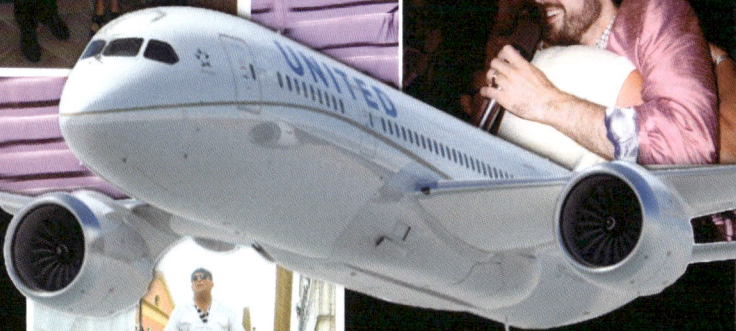

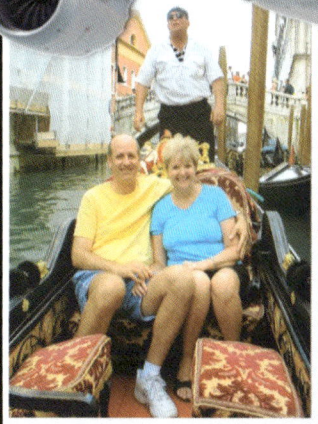

Top Left: I was fortunate
to meet Donny & Marie
in 2007

Right: I hugged Donny
Osmond in 1983

Bottom: Venice, Italy
June   2009

Chapter 9
God Has a Plan … I Have a Plan … My Plan Doesn't Count!
♥

I really don't know how people who do not have a higher being in their life make it. As a little girl, I remember attending church and Sunday school. Most people can tell you the exact time and place that they were when they accepted Jesus Christ into their lives. I really don't know the exact time or place; I don't remember ever *not* believing in a powerful God.

As a baby, I was dedicated in the Sandy Valley Church of God. It was the family church of my mom's family. My Grandma Marlor is the person that comes to my mind when I think of a wonderful

Christian lady. She was a great role model who practiced what she believed in at all times.

When I moved to Tennessee, I shopped around for churches. It was very hard moving to a new state and not knowing a soul other than my husband at the time. I found the perfect fit for me at Greenville United Methodist Church in Joelton, Tennessee. I have been a member there for 24 years.

My decision to join the church was an easy one. I chose to be baptized as an adult by Brother John Meadors when I changed churches. I feel as though God has taught me that I am special at an early age. I may not have been granted 20/20 vision, but I have been blessed with so many other wonderful qualities.

First, I am blessed to have been born to parents that loved me and encouraged me to be all that I could be. God granted me wonderful hearing, perception, and organizational skills to be able to do anything I set my mind out to do. He also gave me the ability to LOVE PEOPLE!

When I was in the first grade, our class had our picture taken. My picture appeared in the class photo twice. Mom said I came home from school and said, "Guess what? I have a twin!" God was showing me I was special even back then.

Recently I have accepted a part-time job working two days a week as an Intervention Specialist in an elementary school. I had to go and be fingerprinted. I was told I had no fingerprint traces. I had to go back a second time. I told Steve, maybe he was married to an angel who didn't need fingerprints … not sure if he bought my story.

When I was principal at East Cheatham Elementary School, I always said that I didn't run the school—God did! No matter what circumstance was happening, things always seemed to work out for the betterment of the students.

♥

The motto I live by is: *God Has a Plan … I Have a Plan … My Plan Doesn't Count!* His timing and plan is always so much better than my own. I have always been a person who loves to be in charge, and needs to know what I am doing next. It has taken me many years to try to practice what I know in my heart is the right thing to do—wait on him.

I was reminded just this morning in my daily devotional reading of his plan. *Commit your way to the Lord; trust in him and he will do this: He will make your righteous reward shine like the dawn, your vindication like the noonday sun. Psalms: 37, 5 & 6*. Yes, God has a greater plan for each of us.

♥

"Jesus Christ"
Painted by Warner
Sallman 1892 - 1968

Chapter 10
Mrs. Good Choice = 20/20
♥

God gives us each talents and gifts to use to the best of our abilities. Although I feel as though I have been granted many gifts in my life, the gift of teaching children to make wise choices and the importance of good character is my true passion.

This journey began when I started my teaching career back in 1986. God did not bless me with birth children of my own. Many times, I questioned his decision, felt sad, and disheartened when all of my friends were having families. However, when I gave up trying to run my own life, it all became clear. God trusted me enough to place thousands of *other* peoples' children in the palms of my hands every year.

As a teacher and elementary school principal, my job was to keep children safe, happy, and help them learn the importance of being honest, trustworthy, respectful, kind, caring, and to teach them how to become good citizens. The key to teaching children is to model *your* expectations first. Children need to see good role models.

One of my life goals was to write a children's book one day. Being a principal was very time consuming. I never had the time or the opportunity to pursue my dream. Suddenly, God had other plans for me!

After my thirteenth year as a principal, I was moved to Central

Office to be a Teacher Improvement Coordinator. At the time, I was sad and confused. East Cheatham Elementary School was my 'home away from home'. The teachers, assistants, cafeteria ladies, custodians, bus drivers, parents, and children were my family.

Once again—God's plan—obviously better than mine. My new job was less stressful and gave me tons of down time. In my down time, I wrote my first children's book, *The ABC's of Making Good Choices*. It came out in October of 2013.

My first book was never sent off to publishers. God placed people in my life at the right time to have it illustrated and published.

The way it happened is a story in itself. I call it a God wink!

♥

That was just the beginning of a new chapter in my life. I decided to write a children's series. The Mrs. Good Choice Series is my new work in progress. My sweet Aunt Sandy is my illustrator. She has never had an art lesson in her life. She is using her God-given talent and her work is amazing.

The series is designed with individuals that foster positive Character Traits: Responsibility, Respect, Honesty, Compassion and much more. Each book provides children with heartfelt stories to help them make good choices and teach them how their choices can affect them in today's world. They give parents and teachers the opportunity and guides available to help open dialogue about positive character traits.

Now that I am retired, I am spending my days writing, making author visits, and learning all about social media. Mrs. Good Choice now has a wonderful website, thanks to Jay Horne. As my publisher, he has helped me establish a Mrs. Good Choice Blog. Mrs. Good Choice is also on Twitter, Facebook, and Pinterest.

My goals for the future include the continuation of the Mrs. Good Choice line of books as well as motivational speaking. I would like to inspire people to find their way to fulfillment in life. If *I* can do it, anyone can. I would like to write future books, as well. Life holds many unknown twists and turns.

If you have a dream and are willing to pursue it, anything can happen!

♥

Mrs. Good Choice

Children's Author
Dawn Young

My Aunt Sandy
Sandra Peshek
Illustrator of Mrs.
Good Choice Series

Performing with Mrs.
Good Choice

Mrs. Good Choice Audience

Chapter 11
You Can Do It!
♥

As I sit and write this last chapter, I want you to know that I have thought about and pondered for many hours the reasons I wanted to share my story. I feel as though God is leading me to put my story in words to help others. My story is still unfolding. Each day brings me new challenges and new rewards.

Here, I would like to tell you a bit about my eye condition. I was born with a missing cell in my optic nerve, and this resulted in nearsightedness, farsightedness, and astigmatism. I am also colorblind when it comes to some colors. I can distinguish red and yellow from green. I mix up the blues, greens, greys, and earth tones. I make sure my clothes match, though. I always ask the salesperson what the color is if I am not sure. A safety pin goes on the tag of all my brown pants so I can tell them from the black ones.

This all gets extremely interesting when playing any card game with colors, such as Uno©. When it comes to telling the blue from the green, it is hilarious for my co-players.

No matter what your own story is, whether you were born with a birth defect, a disability, born into an economically disadvantaged family, developed a rare disease or illness, have overcome a drug or alcohol addiction, know that you are not alone. God sacrificed his son Jesus Christ to save us. All you have to do is ask for his help. I am reminded of a lovely passage that I would like to share with you now. *"Behold, I stand at the door and knock; if any man hears my voice, and opens the door, I will come in to him." Revelations 3:20.* As he tells us, all we have to do is ask.

There are no rules, guidelines, or restrictions. I know that I am blessed beyond what I deserve. I have a wonderful husband, parents, family, and hundreds of friends. Am I still legally blind? Absolutely! I would like to change the (_We to I_) in this passage in scripture. *We live by faith, not by sight. 2 Corinthians 5:7.*

I want to encourage you to follow your dreams. Don't ever give up and think you can't do it. I am here to tell you that *you* can be anything you want to be and do anything you want to do with hard work, perseverance, and prayer.

If my story makes a difference in one person's life, then I made a difference—blessings to you and your story.

♥

Scriptures taken from The Holy Bible, New International Version, NIV© 1973, 1978, 1984, 2011 by Biblical Inc. Published by Zondervan, Grand Rapids, MI 49530, USA

Dawn Renee Cowley Young
Ashland City, Tennessee
April 2015

"Heart's Door"
Painted By Warner
Sallman 1892 - 1968

ABOUT THE AUTHOR: DAWN YOUNG

Dawn is a retired Teacher, Principal, and Teacher Improvement Coordinator. She has been actively publishing the Mrs. Good Choice children's line of books. She is continuing her journey of taking her one lady educational program, "Good Choices Matter" into schools and libraries. Look for her next publication coming soon in the Mrs. Good Choice book series. Dawn lives with her family in Tennessee.

To learn more about Dawn Young and her work, please visit **www.mrsgoodchoice.com**

♥

CPSIA information can be obtained at www.ICGtesting.com
Printed in the USA
LVIW01n1406010515
436835LV00001B/1